THE BLACK TORTOISE

THE BLACK TORTOISE

RONALD TIERNEY

RAVEN BOOKS
an imprint of
ORCA BOOK PUBLISHERS

Library and Archives Canada Cataloguing in Publication

Tierney, Ronald, author
The black tortoise / Ronald Tierney.
(Rapid reads)

Issued in print and electronic formats.
ISBN 978-1-4598-1240-6 (paperback).—ISBN 978-1-4598-1241-3 (pdf).—
ISBN 978-1-4598-1242-0 (epub)

I. Title. II. Series: Rapid reads
PS3570.I3325B53 2017   813'.54   C2016-904531-5
C2016-904532-3

First published in the United States, 2017
Library of Congress Control Number: 2016950244

Summary: In this work of crime fiction, forensic accountant Peter
Strand investigates an arts-oriented nonprofit. (RL 4.8)

*Orca Book Publishers is dedicated to preserving the environment and has
printed this book on Forest Stewardship Council® certified paper.*

Orca Book Publishers gratefully acknowledges the support for
its publishing programs provided by the following agencies:
the Government of Canada through the Canada Book Fund and the
Canada Council for the Arts, and the Province of British Columbia
through the BC Arts Council and the Book Publishing Tax Credit.

Cover design by Jenn Playford
Cover photography by iStock.com

ORCA BOOK PUBLISHERS
www.orcabook.com

Printed and bound in Canada.

20 19 18 17 • 4 3 2 1

I heard the water lapping at the pilings.
I went to the edge and looked over. To my
surprise there was a large tortoise—more
likely a turtle, since it was at home in the sea.
Its dark, shiny shell might have been five feet
long. When our eyes met, it disappeared.

ONE

I'm a little bit of a puzzle, I'm afraid. I look Chinese. That's because I'm half Chinese and half Cherokee. Unfortunately, I never knew my parents, a story for later maybe. I was adopted by an elderly white couple from Phoenix. I speak English, no Chinese. But in keeping with the stereotype, I'm very good at math. I became an accountant, one who specializes in forensic accounting. This means I investigate criminals, people who try to cook the books. I also acquired a private investigator's license when I moved to San Francisco.

I've never met Mr. Lehr, though he is my major client. I talk to him on the phone or we converse by email. He is an important man in the city. He owns a lot of property, from which he earns a handsome living. I help him by looking into his investments for signs of fraud, embezzlement or kickbacks—any criminal behavior tied to the handling of money. My private investigator's license allows me to look into past behavior and associations of people with whom Mr. Lehr does or might do business.

I was talking to him when a riotous band of wild parrots swooped into a berry-bearing tree outside my bedroom deck. They screeched as they battled over the fruit. I barely heard Mr. Lehr, who was speaking in low tones, obviously trying not to be overheard.

"Strand, listen," he said in a gravelly whisper. "You know the Fog City Arts Center?"

I did. From what I could remember, the center was on a couple of old piers off the Embarcadero along the San Francisco Bay. The buildings housed a couple of theaters and major exhibition space.

"I'm on their board," Lehr said. "Some crazy shit is going on down here. The staff is ready to mutiny. I told the board you'd go down, look into things."

"What things?"

"The crazy stuff. You need to see Madeline Creighton. She's the executive director. So arrange things and straighten it out."

How was I to know the crazy shit he mentioned *was* Madeline Creighton?

—

The business offices of the Black Tortoise Foundation were toward the end of one of two long piers that jutted into San Francisco Bay. I walked along the edge of one of the piers, a distance longer than a football field. The water was choppy. A fleet of pelicans flew in a V-formation within a few feet of the entrance at the far end, where I stood for a moment to get my bearings. I thought about the disorderly parrots, comparing them to the disciplined pelicans and their flight.

I had to wait. Mrs. Madeline Creighton wasn't quite ready for me. As it turned out, I wasn't quite ready for Madeline. She was tall, all bones, cosmetics and jewelry. She jangled when she walked or motioned with her heavily braceleted wrists. When she spoke, every pause turned into a pose, as if she expected to be photographed. I sat in front of her grand desk in a low-slung chair. The setup was designed so the guest would have to look up to her. The walls were covered with photographs of Mrs. Creighton with celebrities from the stage, screen and politics.

"I don't have time to bother with these petty problems," she said, her hands flung wide in dismissal. "You need to talk with Emelio," she said.

"Who is Emelio?" I asked.

"The money man," she said. "That's what all this foolishness is about, isn't it?"

"That is correct. Mr. Lehr talked to you about this?"

"Yes." She smiled. "He said that you were Chinese and very good with numbers."

"He's half right."

"Where in China?"

"Phoenix."

"Where are your parents from?" she asked. Her tone was stern. She didn't like to be played with.

"Scottsdale." I decided not to make it easy for her. "Now if you'll direct me to the money man, I'll take my abacus and go."

***

"Mr. Salazar?

"Emelio," he said.

His clothes were not expensive. His shirt, a little too brightly colored for my taste, was open at the neck, showing a tuft of hair and a gold chain with a cross.

We shook hands, and I was guided to a small table where we sat across from each other.

"You're the money man, she said."

"Madeline prefers to deal with creative people. To her, money is dirty unless you have a lot of it and might give it to her. Having to count it is pedestrian."

Emelio Salazar's office was quite different from Madeline Creighton's. It was furnished with desks and chairs from discount stores, as most nonprofits are. There was a lonely orchid on a file cabinet near the window. A seagull, obviously traveling alone, effortlessly glided by outside the window. I looked around while Emelio fiddled with his computer. Not only were there no celebrity photos—there were no photos at all. Nothing personal. Nothing revealing.

He printed out a page and handed it to me. It was the organization chart. He explained that the foundation, Black Tortoise, managed the Fog City Arts Center for the city's Port Commission. After the costs of running it were deducted from the revenue, the net income went to the commission. It used these funds to maintain the two piers—seismic safety and repair of damage done by water, wind and salt. It was very expensive to keep these old piers from falling apart.

"What are the revenue streams?"

"Rent mostly," he said. "Organizations rent the theaters and the exhibition hall. The space can be divided up into almost any size for conferences, art shows, fund-raising events, celebratory dinners. We contract by amount of space and number of days."

"Anything else?"

"Donations, endowments, as well as interest on investments and the endowments. We're allowed to keep an operating fund that exceeds our anticipated needs. The board members make annual contributions, mostly token. We provide services—equipment, box office and so on—and take a cut of the client's revenue."

"And you look after it all?" I asked. It was more complicated than I thought.

"I reconcile accounts payable and receivable."

"Payable includes payroll, I'm sure. What else?"

"Certainly that's included. We also pay for catering services for our clients—we bill them for the cost of the service plus a markup. That's both payable and receivable. We also have to pay for things like a new boiler or to fix a roof. Money comes in, money goes out. I count it."

"And you are audited?"

"An outside firm. And we pass with flying colors. I'm always prepared. I'm proud of that. In fact, the audit firm often sends its junior auditors to us, because, for all practical purposes, I help train them."

"You are a CPA?" I asked. It wasn't a requirement for being a director of finance.

"Yes. Passed all four tests first time through."

The tests were comparable to passing the bar for lawyers.

"Would you give me access to the financials for the last two years?" I asked him.

He didn't blink. "Sure. I can make some disks for you tonight, get them to you tomorrow."

"Emelio, aren't you one bit curious about who I am, what I'm looking for and why I'm looking for it?"

"What I know is that Mad Madeline has an enemy—one of many, I suspect—on the board, and he sent you to make sure everything is legal. I'm fine with that." He scribbled something on a sticky note and gave it to me. "I'm having an open house tomorrow. My lover and I have a new house, and it's finally ready to show." Emelio touched my hand. "No gifts. There'll be plenty of food and drink. A few members of the staff and some friends. Drop in. I'll introduce you around, and I'll have what you want ready for you. If you get bored, you can sneak out with the disks. Who knows? Maybe Mr. or Ms. Right will be there. Unless you're already caught, you'd be quite a catch for someone."

Thank goodness being a nerd was no longer totally unfashionable.

TWO

I sat outside on my deck with a glass of wine and used Google Maps to find the home Emelio and his friend had just purchased. It was snuggled between Diamond Heights and Twin Peaks. Not a bad neighborhood, but then, there are few bad neighborhoods in San Francisco these days. Even so, this was quite a home for the employee of a nonprofit foundation of Black Tortoise's size, even a director of finance. There were possible explanations. Emelio's lover could be well heeled. Maybe Emelio's family was wealthy. Maybe he'd won the lottery. But an expensive home is always a red flag.

I emailed Emelio and asked if he could insert in his package a list of employees, Madeline included. I requested their job descriptions and salaries. I also asked for bios of senior staff. I wasn't sure what I was looking for, so I wasn't at all sure where to focus my investigation.

The open house was a catered affair—all Mediterranean cuisine, appropriate for the exceptionally sunny and warm San Francisco day. Emelio led me up the steps to an open living space filled with chattering guests holding wineglasses.

"Let me give you the tour first," Emelio said.

It didn't take long. The house was smaller than I'd imagined from the outside. There were only two bedrooms up.

The ground floor, where I had entered, contained another bedroom and the garage, where a plain Honda Civic was parked. The two bedrooms were pleasant but had the feeling of a staged home. In no bedroom were there any telltale signs of real inhabitants. No photos of family or vacations, no books, nothing eccentric, nothing purely sentimental. There was no sense that real people living real lives lived here.

The home, as was increasingly the case in the city's newer houses, had been designed to feature the kitchen. And the kitchen was something to behold. I'm not an expert on kitchens, but I knew the appliance brands were high-end. The countertop was marble.

"I've had to do nothing. A house in financial distress—I got it for a song. But look at these floors!" He was exuberant and conspiratorial at the same time. It was true though. On the second level, the floors in all the rooms were covered in the same dark, expensive-looking hardwood.

"Oh, I lied," he said, touching my arm as we came back through the kitchen and the chattering guests. "I replaced the sink. It was aluminum. And aluminum smudges so easily. And the water marks! Every splatter, every drop. It drove me crazy."

If he had said the kitchen had never been used, I would have believed him. Everything was so tidy—even the trash containers, which were strategically placed for the guests. They were lined with black trash bags and tied in place with white ribbons.

"Do I get to meet your..." I stumbled, searching for the word. Was it companion, lover, husband, other half? "Partner?" I should have been used to this by now. This is the most liberated city in the country. As an Arizona transplant I was surprised at the guests. I had expected an abundance of gays and lesbians, given Emelio's flamboyant manner. But looking at the diversity of the attendees, it could have been a meeting of the United Nations.

Emelio gave me a practiced sad face. He moved closer, almost nose to nose, his eyes on mine as if we had been best friends forever.

"We had a little spat, and, well, Patrick was too upset to deal with all these people. Speaking of people, let me introduce you to some of the guests. Many of them are from work, and you'll want to talk with them anyway."

He took my arm and led me to an athletic-looking man wearing a coral-colored golf shirt. "This is Craig Anglim and his friend Mira. Craig is the director of sales and marketing."

I shook hands. Craig had blond and gray curly hair. His companion was in a short black gown complementing her short, very black hair. "They have three lovely children," Emelio added. He stepped back and looked at me. "Peter is a consultant for someone interested in how Fog City Arts Center operates."

Craig Anglim looked puzzled, but he didn't follow up. We all smiled our good-byes as I was taken to a short fiftyish woman with cropped silver hair. Marguerite Woodson. She wore jeans and a sweatshirt.

"Marge, this is Peter," Emelio said. Marge didn't look happy. "Marge is in charge of operations." Then, to her: "Peter is checking out our auditors, so he'll be going over the books."

"About time," Marge said.

"Marge is an architect and oversees all major construction, repairs and so on." She gave me a civil smile and him a scowl.

"She's a tough old bird," Emelio said as we moved on. "She and Mad Madeline are destined for a serious collision."

"Why?"

"Marge is all about safety and preserving the historic features of the structure. Madeline is all about how things look and not spending money if you can't see what the money bought. Kind of like the way straight men feel about buying underwear and socks.

"One more," Emelio continued, leading me toward an attractive, young woman with long blond hair. Her Latin-looking male companion wore a blazer, white shirt and jeans. A kind of casual, non-revealing, socially acceptable uniform, much like mine.

"This is Vanessa Medder and her friend Jorge Medina. Vanessa is our client liaison. She's involved with all the events that take place at the center while they are happening. She keeps our clients happy."

"And everyone else," said someone from a nearby group of guests.

Jorge Medina said something in Spanish to Emelio. They both laughed.

"Jorge is one of those Silicon Valley guys. A programming genius. Be nice to him. He can make a computer do anything he wants. He'll be a billionaire in no time."

Medina smiled broadly, extending his hand.

Emelio turned to present me.

"Peter has been hired to go over our procedures to make sure we are as efficient and productive as we can be."

"Nice to meet you," I said to the couple, and to Emelio I said I needed to be on my way and that I had a lot to do before Monday.

We moved toward the stairs.

"I didn't see Madeline," I said.

"She wouldn't have come. No one important in attendance. Besides, if she showed up, the party would be over. She isn't exactly beloved." Emelio took a deep breath.

"What do you think of Jorge? Gorgeous, isn't he?"

"They make quite a couple," I said.

"A walk on the wild side, if you ask me," Emelio said. He raised his eyebrows in what he was imagining as a meeting of like-minded souls. "Sizzle," he said. "I can't imagine what goes on in their bedroom." He grinned. Touched my forearm. "Oh yes I can—and do. You are too quiet, Peter."

Emelio wasn't going to give up on pigeonholing me. It killed him not to know. For some reason that gave me pleasure. I looked back at the crowd. Vanessa was whispering something in Jorge's ear. If they were sweet nothings, his serious expression didn't show it.

"Wait here," Emelio said, leaving me at the top of the stairs.

He was gone for only a second. He returned with a large expandable file.

He handed it to me as if he were handing me the secrets of the Da Vinci Code.

"You told each of them a different story about why I am here," I told him.

"I did, didn't I? It will give them a lot to talk about." He laughed. He was in good spirits for someone whose lover had just walked out on him. "Patrick will be sorry he missed you."

"Nice house," I said. Despite the brevity of my visit, I had accomplished quite a bit, thanks to Emelio Salazar, who seemed to be able to read my mind.

"Thank you. See you Monday."

THREE

Much like Emelio's, my home was relatively modern in a city full of Victorian and Edwardian homes. I had two floors, each one with a deck that had dramatic views of the city. I was able to purchase it largely because I did so years ago, through the generosity of my stepparents and what was left to me in the will of my stepfather, who was last to die. I could maintain it because of the regular paycheck from my best and most demanding client, Mr. Lehr. Never mind that I had put myself in a position of well-paid slave.

Even though I was technically self-employed, I was not free. None of us are. We are rarely even free to be ourselves on our own time. To survive, to make a living, we must care how others see us and act accordingly.

So here it was, Saturday afternoon, and an exciting world-class city lay before me. Yet I would use the rest of the day and evening, as well as all day Sunday, to go over the disks Emelio had given me. I would examine the accounts—money received and paid—trying to understand the business. And looking for something that didn't add up. I'm not really complaining. If I had free time, I wouldn't know what to do with it.

I used my laptop and my desktop computers. By Sunday afternoon I had isolated areas of big money, but I found nothing wrong. I reminded myself that the foundation had successfully gone through intense, highly professional outside audits. There was a trained team going over the numbers. I printed out some of what Emelio had given me. I was especially interested in the material on the foundation's various managers. There was Vanessa, client liaison, Craig, the sales director, Marguerite, the architect and operations director, as well as Emelio. And, of course, the top dog, Madeline.

I had resisted the call of the wine bottle while I looked at numbers, to prevent even the slightest blurring. However, I gave in before the sun went down. As I began to read the bios of the main staff and their job descriptions, I sipped some cool white wine. I read and sometimes reread the material until hunger refused to be ignored. I spent the evening hours googling the foundation staff. If I had a life, I missed it.

Coffee at sunrise. Both of my outdoor decks faced east. Sometimes that meant a clear view of the silver San Francisco skyline.

This morning it meant I would stare at a bank of impenetrable fog in the chilly wet air.

I have a car, but I rarely use it unless I'm leaving the city. I took the twisty walking route down the hill. This eventually led to the Saturn Steps, a long, steep stairway leading to relatively flat earth and Market Street. At Market, I hopped on the MUNI, the underground train that would take me through and under the spiky, mountainous high-rises to the Embarcadero and eventually the Black Tortoise Foundation.

A good walk clears the brain, I've found. I realized that Emelio had already introduced me, at his party, to the key players. The family-oriented sales guy Craig Anglim, the attractive events overseer Vanessa Medder and down-to-earth architect Marguerite Woodson. These were the people I most wanted to interview. These three—five including Madeline and

Emelio—were in the best position to access substantial amounts of money. Had Emelio read my mind, or was this simply the way accountants' minds work? A yes answer to either question would be scary. I didn't find the idea of Emelio and I having similar characteristics encouraging.

The doors to the foundation were locked. The hours of operation painted on the glass doors told me I was fifteen minutes early.

I heard the water lapping at the pilings. I went to the edge and looked over. To my surprise there was a large tortoise— more likely a turtle, since it was at home in the sea. Its dark, shiny shell might have been five feet long. When our eyes met, it disappeared.

What a strange creature. A living being with its own mobile home. The moment it is observed, it hides—in the ocean or in its shell. We can see it, but only as much as it wants us to see. As is the case with all of us, it cannot completely ignore reality. But it can withdraw from it more than most of us can.

Farther out in the bay, beneath the low-hanging fog, was a cormorant. The long-necked bird floated—bobbed, really—on the slightly rough waters. Suddenly it dove under, disappeared. There I stood, inches from another world, yet always a little separate from it.

"Aren't you freezing to death?" Emelio asked. He was the first human I'd seen trudge down the pier. There were seagulls and pigeons walking before him, getting out of his way. He wore gloves and a thick scarf. It was wrapped around his neck several times. "You must come from Mongolia," he said to me.

"Hearty stock," I said. "Will Madeline be in today?" I asked as he unlocked the door.

"Hard to tell. She lives in her own world." He flipped on the lights. A phone rang. "I'm so tired," he said, drawing out the words to heighten the drama. "After the guests left, Patrick came home all apologetic and affectionate. No sleep. It was worth the spat. Know what I mean?"

Once he stopped fidgeting with the lights, I gave him a list of the people I needed to see. He would arrange it as best he could, he said. I was given a small conference room in which to conduct business. I watched a news channel on my laptop until the first staff member arrived at 9:30 AM.

Marge Woodson appeared not to have changed clothes since Emelio's party on Saturday. The other possibility was that blue jeans, gray sweatshirt and sneakers were a kind of personal uniform. I saw her roll her bicycle into her office as I went for coffee in the kitchenette.

I wasn't surprised that she had pedaled in from way out at Ocean Beach. But I was surprised and deeply impressed to learn that she participated in an annual swim to Alcatraz. Her educational background was impressive too. Her work experience tended toward restoration and eco-friendly solutions to restoration problems.

"Of all the people here, you spend the most money," I said to her. I was intentionally abrupt. I wanted to see her reaction to a subtle accusation.

"Yes," she said, leaning forward in her chair, "but my spending preserves history and maintains safety. It's not frivolous."

"Unlike?" I knew she was mad at someone.

"Our dear leader," she said. I waited for her to continue. "Madeline had her office soundproofed. She took one of my workmen without asking. She had him put in all new studs, insulation and drywall to make sure no one could hear what was going on in her office. What is this, the CIA? She took him off an important job. She didn't talk to me about it. She had him install security cameras in and outside the office and put a buzzer release on the door. Why? Nobody hates us. We're not controversial. We do good work here. Well, we did."

She took a deep breath and shook her head.

"Then suddenly, after the cameras were installed, she changed her mind about them. She may have realized she was the only person who had something to hide."

"They've never been turned on?"

She shook her head again. "The foundation also paid for her move from the east coast when they hired her. The city is full of qualified people—*more* qualified people."

Marguerite had to have learned this from Emelio, I thought. He enjoyed stirring things up.

"Does anyone like her?"

"No. She's a uniting force in that regard. We may have problems with one another from time to time, but we all hate her."

"Don't hold back," I said.

She laughed. It was deep and hearty. "I don't know who you are or what your game is, so I may be committing professional suicide, but I'm beyond caring. Someone is going to get killed by falling concrete, or they'll fall in the bay and drown. And she's frittering away the budget on whatever little whim crosses her tiny brain."

"What about the board?"

"What about them? The previous director was doing fine. The board let him go. We don't know why. They hired a search firm, paid them a fortune. They spent I don't know how many months looking for an executive director and ended up with…"

"Mad Madeline."

"Off With Their Heads Madeline. We're all one temper tantrum away from the streets."

"Maybe that's why she wants sound-proofing and a security system."

"Maybe. What's your interest in all this?" she asked.

"I think maybe some members of the board want to know what's going on."

"They're not the only ones."

FOUR

It was clear Craig Anglim didn't want to make waves. He squirmed in his seat even before the questions about his co-workers began, especially about Mad Madeline. He wouldn't touch the subject. Instead, he suggested a tour of the two piers—the rental space.

It was a good idea. Revenue from the space was substantial. The two theaters could be used in conjunction with the vast open spaces or separately. The same with the piers. Both or just one. Each pier could be customized for specific purposes.

They had had art shows, product launches, association conventions, wine tastings, Craig explained.

"And you rent to anyone?" I asked as we entered the larger of the two theaters.

"The philosophy used to be 'to anyone or anything, as long as it's legal.'"

"Now?" I asked.

"Well," he said, looking around as if someone might save him, "the new executive director has to okay it."

"Madeline?"

"Yes. She wants to raise the quality of the clientele."

"You've lost business?"

"Some," he said.

"Are you and your salespeople paid a commission?"

"A bonus based on how much we exceed expectations." He looked down for a moment, then hurried ahead, into a theater.

"Now this theater has three hundred seats. It's perfect for independent dance companies," he said, clearly trying to change the subject. "And sometimes we can help small companies get grants to help them pay the rent."

"Everyone handles their own ticket sales?"

"Oh no," he said. "We handle the box office for all events having an admission price. It's a requirement."

"And you take a cut?"

"The foundation does, yes. A straight fee to do it and a percentage of the gate. We set it up in the contract. The events-management people look after it."

"Vanessa?"

"Yes."

I still had Vanessa, Emelio and Madeline to interview before my day and perhaps my job was done. Emelio suggested a lunch interview with him after I'd talked to Vanessa. Madeline was scheduled for two o'clock.

Vanessa's staff were on call. "Big event, lots of staff," she explained. "Small event, minimal staff.

"During big art shows, we have thousands of people come through here. There are hundreds of booths, food and wine. We have to keep it clean and safe. For example, we have to make sure that exits aren't blocked, trash bins are emptied, computers work, the lighting is right. It goes on," she said, flipping her long blond hair. "And we watch our suppliers—caterers, equipment and furniture providers—if applicable."

"Is there a markup?"

"Yes, but sales sets all of that up. Once we get close to an event, we take over from sales. In the end, we provide the info for billing."

"You also handle the box office."

"Yes, but that's pretty automatic. It's a program. A full reconciliation is provided to the client and to our own finance department. The report is computer generated. It's a breeze. Actually, our clients like it when they realize how much it simplifies their events."

"How have you been affected by your new boss, Madeline?"

She looked at me warily. "She's interested in the theater. That's her background. Unless we expect famous attendees, she leaves us alone."

"She doesn't show up?

"She's busy. She's a very busy person."

"Doing what?"

"I have no idea."

Sometimes work is boring. I'm not a people person. I prefer it when the numbers tell the story. That's my training. But the numbers weren't saying much. As I kept reminding myself, the foundation was audited by a reputable firm. And they had seen nothing even remotely questionable. In fact, the foundation had passed its audits with flying colors for the past five years. The firm's letter to the foundation's audit and finance committee was uncharacteristically enthusiastic. Emelio was doing an impeccable job, it seemed. But I still had some serious questions.

FIVE

Emelio and I had lunch at the Ferry Building. The huge building, also on the bay, has been spectacularly restored. There are still ferries that carry tourists and commuters to and from places on the vast San Francisco Bay. But the Ferry Building has been reconfigured to house shops and restaurants. The world-famous Vietnamese restaurant Slanted Door occupies one end. Another restaurant with a large outdoor space for dining occupies the other end. In between, there are specialty food shops. If you want mushrooms, there is a shop with all sorts of the fungi. Whether you want bread, cheese, crab, gelato, wine, tea, kitchen stuff, chocolate, flowers or coffee, the choices are unlimited. There is a Japanese delicatessen, a Mexican restaurant and a joint specializing in fresh seafood.

We ended up at the big outdoor restaurant, with two glasses of chilled white wine. There was a calmer-than-usual sea breeze and blue skies. To the right of us was a line of fresh produce stands. In front of us, across the wide Embarcadero, was the financial district. It is a large gathering of high-rises housing international corporations, especially those connected to the Pacific Rim economy.

After the waiter took our order I began my questions.

"You said you were a certified public accountant...?"

He didn't need the whole question. He was ready to answer it. He wasn't the least bit unnerved.

"It's easier that way," Emelio said, smiling. "I received my accountancy training in London. I'm a qualified accountant through the CCAB—the Consultative Committee of Accountancy Bodies. I'm also a chartered accountant. To explain it is confusing and boring. So I just say I'm a CPA."

Technically he wasn't a CPA, but he had gained a license in Europe with similar requirements. It wasn't confusing, but it *was* boring, so I moved on.

"Older records show that you were once the executive director of the Black Tortoise Foundation."

He took a sip of wine. "A little more than a year ago. I was the acting executive director. The board couldn't find anyone. They formed a search committee. After many months they narrowed it to three candidates. By that time I was already out of the race. One withdrew, and it became a choice between two crazy ladies. They chose one."

"Were you considered?"

"Not seriously."

"Why not?"

"One member of the board told me in private that they were looking for someone who presented well. Someone with authority, someone people took seriously."

"You did apply?"

"I did. I was here—I had a proven record. While I was in charge, everything ran like a top. But what they saw was this short, obviously gay man who appears uncomfortable in a public setting."

"Surely a gay executive director for an arts center in San Francisco wouldn't be a problem."

"No," he said softly. He seemed to freeze and his eyes darted about. "But some gay guys are impressive, very successful. Many have a knack for commanding respect. I guess I'm a behind-the-scenes kind of guy.

"So Madeline takes over," I said, to change the focus.

"They paid big-time to find her. Paid even more to move her," he said, obviously relieved to move on. "They paid her for three months *before* she got here. They put her up in a fancy hotel for three more months, until she found a home. I know. I wrote the checks. She's cost us a fortune. Her management skills? Expenses are up, revenue is down. She actually turns away clients."

"I heard. Yet Craig had nothing bad to say about her."

Emelio leaned forward across the table. It was the intimate gossip pose. He was at home now. "Craig is having an affair. A divorce is imminent. Three children. That means child support, a mortgage and rent. He can't afford to lose his job.

And Madeline demonstrated early on that she will fire people on the spot. She's usually locked away in her office. But when the door opens, people scatter like cockroaches when someone hits the light switch. They go out of their way to avoid her."

"Weren't Craig and his wife at your house for the party?"

"That was his girlfriend. And I'm sure that in her own way, she probably costs a pretty penny too."

"What does Madeline think about her employees avoiding her?"

"She may not notice. She's very self-absorbed." He smiled coyly, understanding that he was also viewed that way. "On the other hand, she may like that she doesn't have to deal with the little people."

"Marge doesn't like her, I take it," I said.

"Marge and I didn't get along until Madeline showed up. She told me she'd like to take Madeline out for a little swim.

44

She's convinced that the heavy, gaudy charm bracelets would take Madeline to the bottom of the bay."

"She took over one of Marge's staff members as her own," I said. A private investigator knows the value of gossip too.

"She did," Emelio said. "Mine too. She's made my IT guy her personal assistant. I mean, the woman couldn't dial a rotary phone. She's constantly having him solve her problems with her personal cell, both her laptops and God knows what else."

"Both her laptops?" I asked.

"One is for foundation business, and one is personal."

The food arrived, and I glanced up. On the median between the traffic lanes of the Embarcadero was a drummer and several skateboarders. Ancient trolleys, one made of wood and restored from past service in Milan, stopped to pick up riders heading to Fisherman's Wharf. People walked by, people who came from all sorts of places around the world, engaged in lives I could not imagine. Another day in paradise, I thought, even though I was now caught up in tawdry, petty gossip. Yes, Emelio and I were more alike than I cared to admit.

It has happened before. I am to do some minor investigation, and suddenly I find myself separated from simple, honest, motiveless accounting. I am drawn into the battle of egos, obsessions and emotions.

"What's the story with Vanessa?"

"Bottle blond," he said, laughing. "Though of course I don't know firsthand." He managed to make his smile dramatically evil.

"Are you gay?" he asked, in the same tone one might use to ask someone to pass the salt. *If all else fails, be direct.*

"Vanessa had nothing unkind to say about Madeline," I asked in place of answering his question.

"I only ask because it's a puzzle. I usually know right away. I'm not coming on to you. Patrick and I are very happy."

"That's great. Perhaps I'll get to meet Patrick sometime," I said. "Emelio, I have a one-track mind. Vanessa?"

"I don't think she and Madeline have much contact. And Vanessa's skill set is dealing with difficult, demanding clients. Insincerity is built into the job description. If you asked her about the Nazis, she'd say something like, 'I'm sure they meant well.' All Madeline really wants is to be worshipped. That's in Vanessa's professional toolbox."

"Doesn't Vanessa oversee the box office?"

"She sets it up. But it's a program. She might step in if there's a glitch, or if the client complains. The program has been in place for quite a while. It's glitch-free. It runs on its own."

I took a bite of my blackened-rock-cod sandwich.

In this interlude, his eyes appraised me as a wild animal might, assessing danger or considering a menu item.

I was uncomfortable and decided to reignite his obvious passion for gossip. "I found some interesting old news stories on Madeline's historic theater company back east," I said.

Emelio poked at his salad. "It seemed pretty shady, but the mayor of that little town took the fall."

"She started a consulting business," I said.

"She and her husband ran it," he added. Emelio had done as much investigating as I had.

"The checks you cut have to have two signatures, right?"

"Mine and hers," Emelio said.

"How interested is Madeline when she signs the checks? Does she ask questions?"

"She doesn't pay attention. I think I could get her to sign my laundry receipt."

It was all very interesting. But it wasn't my job to criticize or make suggestions about effective management techniques or job qualifications beyond the financial sphere. My plan was to meet with Madeline at two and wrap it up for Mr. Lehr. I would tell him there were serious morale and management problems, but that financially, I saw nothing illegal.

"You have a beautiful home," I told Emelio to guide the conversation toward a comfortable area while we finished lunch.

He beamed. "I was so lucky. The owners couldn't pay their mortgage, and it was right before the housing market exploded again. Timing is everything. Patrick and I were getting more serious, and he had some funds tucked away."

On the walk back he said, "You might have guessed it, but my youth was pretty rough. People beat me up. I was headed in the wrong direction, destined to be a loser, a nobody like the rest of my family. But look at me now. I travel. I have a fine job, a great house, a handsome lover."

"Now all you need is to get the executive director's job," I said, only half joking.

He smiled. "Think positive, I say."

Madeline's door was open. Emelio waved enthusiastically as I approached the dragon's den. We were fast friends now, co-conspirators.

Madeline wasn't at her desk. She was across the room, staring into an ornate mirror.

"Scientists believe that humans aren't the only animals who are self-aware," I said.

She turned and looked right through me. I wasn't there.

"We have an appointment at two," I said.

"You're the accountant," she said, making me as inconsequential as possible.

"The *forensic* accountant," I said.

She gave me a second, more serious glance. She understood the difference.

"I can't possibly see you today. I have things to do." The words were clear, but the tone had a *pity me* kind of quality.

"I'm about done here," I said. "I can leave the rest to the attorneys and investigators. I had hoped I could close this out myself."

She walked around behind her desk.

"I'm sorry. I overcommitted. It's not easy turning this place around. It's like a battleship. I get no cooperation. Be a saint and give me until tomorrow morning. Could you possibly come back then?" She was acting more and more forlorn. "Maybe early. At eight, before things get crazy. I promise to give you my full attention."

"I'd be honored."

I'm pretty sure she thought I meant it.

The morning was a replay of the previous day's. The fog hung low. There was a chill in the air. I wished I had worn something that would block the cold, wet wind from cutting through me. The office was locked. I walked to the end of the pier and leaned carefully over the railing, the top of which was now missing. I thought I might see the sea turtle again.

Something was there, all right. And at first I thought it was my little shelled creature—turtle or tortoise—with a shiny black shell, but it was a plastic rain slicker. What it covered could have been almost anything, I suppose. But I was pretty sure it was a body. My belief was confirmed when the choppy water flipped up the slicker and I made out a face bobbing lifelessly. It was as if the pale corpse were shedding a second skin or emerging from its shell.

I called 9-1-1. As I provided the operator with information and answered her questions, I saw Marge. She was in a helmet, walking her bicycle along the pier toward my discovery and me. I motioned for her to speed things up. She did.

She came alongside and leaned her bike against the pier. I pointed down.

"Oh God," she said, her voice a mix of surprise and horror. "It's David."

She looked at the damaged railing. "I knew this would happen."

She closed her eyes for a moment, to gather strength or calm herself or both. She went through her bag, pulling out keys. I told her I had called it in. She opened the office and disappeared inside. The sirens had begun and were getting louder. I waited. Marge reappeared with a long pole.

"What are you doing? I asked. If this was no accident, she was disturbing evidence.

There was no thought of rescue. He was dead.

"Just making sure David doesn't float away." Her face was still rosy from the bike ride, but she was upset, clearly upset. *Maybe I should go in and get him.* She moved toward the edge—to shimmy down to the body, I figured.

"No, the fire department is coming. I hear them." I also heard the whooping police sirens, slightly out of tune and out of sync with the wailing fire-engine sirens.

"David works here?" I asked.

"He's IT—the computer guy."

She took charge, guiding the firefighters, the EMTs and the police when they arrived.

I was a little lost, I admit. What could I do? I knocked on Madeline's office door. I heard a muffled "What is it?" The door opened. She looked out into the crowded office, at the madness of it. She pulled me inside and shut the door behind me.

"What's going on?" she asked.

"Your computer guy…"

"Yes?" she asked with impatience.

"David has been found dead in the bay."

She looked up at the ceiling, no doubt seeing into God's private office. "Why does everything happen to me?"

The door opened. Marge was with a large and somewhat intimidating black woman who wore a conservative but stylish gray flannel suit.

"This is Inspector Hadley from the San Francisco Police Homicide Detail," Marge said.

Hadley moved toward Madeline's desk.

"You're homicide?" Madeline asked in a tone of disbelief.

"No, I'm a meter maid," Hadley said, her voice dripping with sarcasm. "Your guest chairs are double-parked."

"I don't have time for this," Madeline said.

"Make time," Hadley said, pulling out a notebook.

"I have a meeting with Mr. Strand."

I had suddenly become important.

"First things first," I said. I was pretty sure Madeline wouldn't be able to charm or intimidate her way out of this one. I didn't leave. I wanted to see this. There was obviously something seriously wrong here. Something more than a little financial pilfering, low morale or inept management. Mr. Lehr was right. He had a nose for these things.

But I was dismissed by Hadley "for the time being" after she noted who I was, how I could be reached and what I was doing there. The office swarmed with foundation staff, huddled in pockets to gossip. Other cops—plainclothes cops—had arrived and were picking off staff one by one for questioning. At one point I looked over and saw Madeline standing in the doorway of her office. She was looking at the confusion as a monarch might if the enemy were suddenly within the walls of her castle.

Vanessa had found a quiet corner and was talking into her cell phone. Marge was talking to her maintenance staff. Craig stood by himself, confused and looking at the chaos. And Emelio had just arrived, cutting through the crowd purposefully.

Outside, uniformed cops, the crime-scene folks and photographers milled about. A sleek police boat had tied up at the end of the pier.

David, the computer guy, was dead. Was it an accident? The broken rail suggested it was, but it wasn't absolutely clear. Negligence was likely though. I called Lehr.

"What do you make of it?" he asked.

"Murder trumps embezzlement and money laundering. Negligence isn't much better."

"Let me know what you find out."

"The police have it now, and you're already paying them."

He laughed. "You have something better to do?"

"It's a matter of qualifications."

"Trust me," Lehr said. "It's about money. It's always about money. And you are the forensic accountant. What do the police know about such things?"

Inspector Hadley caught up with me as I got to the curb of the Embarcadero. I was going to hail a cab, an unusual act for me because public transportation was quick and cheap, but I suddenly felt exhausted. Death can be draining, even if it isn't yours.

"I thought I told you to stick around," she said.

"You told me you'd get to me later. It was a little vague."

"Let's compromise. Now is later. Let's talk," she said, no longer scolding. "What brought you here to investigate?"

I've told her, and she wanted to know what I had concluded.

"I found nothing so far."

"Any thoughts about who might have killed David?"

"You think it's murder?" I asked.

"Don't know yet. Could be an accident. He leaned against the rail. It gave. He fell in. Couldn't swim."

"You don't buy it," I said.

"I don't do anything at the moment. What about you? What do you know now that you didn't know when you started? For example, what do you know about the victim?"

"I didn't even talk with David. I talked with four of the top five in management, the people with access to money or who could conceivably get kickbacks. I didn't see where David had that opportunity. There were no recent major computer purchases nor any such plans in next year's budget. Other than this special relationship with Madeline, I know nothing about him."

"A special relationship?" Hadley asked.

"She needed a lot of help with her computer, her phone and anything else digital."

"And David supplied it? So...?"

"You'll have to supply what comes after *so*."

"Take a stab at it," Hadley said.

"She took up a lot of his time. She didn't seem to care that David reported to Emelio and that he had responsibilities other than being her guide in the digital universe."

"You didn't bother questioning him though?"

I felt chastised. Guilty. Hadley walked back toward the scene of the crime. I flagged a taxi. I thought Hadley smart and suspected she'd do a good job on the investigation. She had me thinking about it all again—she and Lehr.

David may not have had much access to money, but he had access to information. Emails, searches, phone calls, texts. In Madeline's case, it appeared David also had access to her personal computer and smartphone. She seemed to have separated two from the herd—the computer guy and the maintenance guy, the man who had soundproofed her office. Both of them could help her keep secrets. What secrets needed protecting?

SIX

I had the taxi drop me off at Zuni Café for lunch. I could do some work at the table, have a decent lunch, maybe a glass of wine, and work it all off walking home.

I was seated in the bar area, by the window that looked out onto Market Street. I ordered the fennel sausage, Japanese eggplant and a glass of wine of the waiter's choosing. Some people race cars. Others grow flowers or collect stamps. I eat. I also work.

I sipped the wine, opened my laptop, clicked on *History* and went to Madeline's old website. The thing was, it wasn't really old. Under *Contact Information*, the phone number had a 415 area code. One of San Francisco's area codes. Was she allowed to keep her old business running while getting a hefty salary to run the Black Tortoise Foundation?

I sent an email to Emelio, asking him to send me Madeline's contract and David's résumé.

Walking is a way I work things out. Today was perfect. The fog had cleared, and after a pleasant lunch I walked Market Street. I reminded myself that David's death might have nothing to do with Mr. Lehr's suspicions. It might have nothing to do with work at all. A jealous lover maybe? A mugging gone wrong? Simply a crazy, random act by a stranger?

The morning's horror had led me to consider David as the possible keeper of a secret—money related or not. And the idea that it wasn't money related opened up too many possibilities. I would, as it was popular to say these days, "follow the money," if I could find it.

I walked up from Market Street to Douglass and then up to the Vulcan Steps, a separate set of steps a block away from but parallel to the Saturn Steps. There were more than a hundred steps—I counted them once—twisting now and then between the houses on the hill. Every time I made this trek I wondered how the residents moved in or out of homes or had refrigerators or sofas delivered. There were no streets, just the long, steep, narrow stairway. Somehow the people who live here found a way. But whatever it was, it probably wasn't easy.

The other thought that passed through my brain as I climbed my way toward home was that the reason I like to solve accounting crimes versus others, such as murder, is that numbers are black and white. You don't have to interpret them.

Given that, I was the wrong investigator for this case, unless there was something a computer wizard could do to mask a redirection of funds. Was that the secret David held? While it was too late to ask David, maybe I could find out what his bank accounts looked like or what might be found where he lived. That he worked for Emelio, the director of finance, as well as being Madeline's chosen slave wasn't lost on me.

I had other questions as well. My mind was buzzing. There would be no nap waiting for me after conquering the steps. I made calls, went through the emails Emelio had sent me earlier. A contact at Immigration and Customs Enforcement (ICE) returned my call. Emelio wasn't a US citizen. He had no green card. My contact assured me that this fact was just between us. I didn't care if Emelio was living here unofficially. Being half Cherokee, I can trace my ancestry back to the original inhabitants, so I could make the case that the majority of US citizens are illegal immigrants. But I did want to check on Emelio's claim of being a qualified accountant.

I also received a copy of Madeline's contract from Emelio. There was nothing specific that forbade her from operating another business. But no court would stand in the way of ousting her on the basis that she was operating her own business on the foundation's property and time. The real kicker, though, was the amount of money the foundation would have to pay to get rid of her.

What Madeline had negotiated was phenomenal. The Fog City Arts Center had completely financed her move from the Atlantic Coast to the Pacific. They had paid her a fortune for creating havoc while she was here. And they would have to provide another fortune for her to leave. An incredible scam. And nothing illegal. She was good. Her lunatic behavior might be part of the plan. Fire the crazy lady before she destroys the entire center. The question was, had she taken even more from the golden goose? And would she murder someone to cover it up?

David's résumé provided his home address. I was fighting the idea of going there. Interfering in an active murder investigation was not in my job description, and it was illegal. On the other hand, I knew things Hadley did not know, and it would take her a while to find out those things unless I offered my help.

SEVEN

"**N**ice wheels," Hadley said, motioning at my old black Mercedes. She was headed toward her unmarked Ford Crown Victoria.

"It's more than forty years old," I told her, to downplay its value and to come across as less snooty.

"So am I," she said.

"Classics both."

"What are you doing here?" she asked, glancing up at the large Victorian house where David roomed. She spoke with enough gruffness to warn me against such smooth talking. I took note.

"Thought maybe we could help each other," I said. "Anything inside David's place?" I looked again at the building to make sure it matched the address on David's résumé.

"Don't play me," she said. "What are you doing here?"

"You know I was hired to find out if someone at the foundation was cooking the books."

"Were they?" she asked. Uniformed police were coming out of the house with a computer and some cardboard storage boxes.

"I had concluded no until I found David floating in the bay."

"Yeah, well, that brings me to the subject of your being first on the scene," she said.

"Are you're saying...?"

"I'm putting you in your place."

"That's an old and unfortunate attitude."
I went back to my car. I could feel my face

burning. I wasn't exactly sure why. It was one thing to remind me it was her job as a homicide detective to work the case. It was another to interpret authority as superiority.

I drove off. Within two blocks, I heard the whooping of a police siren. I pulled over and rolled down my window. My stepfather had told me it was proper to stay in the car and wait for instructions.

She came to the window. She said nothing.

"Lights, sirens...I'm impressed with your toys of intimidation."

She laughed. "Let's start over."

We went to a coffeehouse on Eighteenth Street on Potrero Hill. All of San Francisco took on a peachy glow below as the sun began to dim.

I told her what I knew, except for Emelio's illegal immigration status. I clearly related how Madeline's immediate staff felt about her.

"I'm surprised she wasn't the one floating in the drink. I'll ask again. Did you talk to David?"

"Maybe I made a mistake, but I couldn't see how he had access to serious money. Then again, Madeline plucked him out to be her personal guide on her computers."

"Computers plural now?"

"Yes. I suspect she was maintaining her consulting business on one while doing her foundation work on the other."

"You confronted her?" Hadley asked.

"I was about to when I saw David floating and then you showed up."

Hadley added to her notes.

"What she was doing was unethical but not illegal," I said.

"But it might have gotten her fired."

"I doubt if she cared about that enough to kill someone."

"You understand the mind of a murderer?" Hadley asked.

I didn't answer. But I was right. Madeline would only have a motive if she was skimming gold from the goose and David was in on it. Hadley and I talked more. I gave her my take on Vanessa, Craig and Marge as potential embezzlers and as satisfied employees. Much of it was gleaned from Emelio's gossip.

As part of our starting over, Hadley said that David lived alone. He had once had a roommate, but San Francisco was too expensive for him, and the guy had moved back to Baltimore. And David was about to be evicted himself. Rents in the city were at a record high.

"Yes," she said, taking a breath and looking around to see if anyone was within earshot. "Given what's left of the railing, engineers have determined that someone just leaning against it wouldn't have caused it to fail."

"Doesn't rule out suicide," I said.

"No, but it makes it unlikely. If he wanted to jump in, he would have climbed over or between the rails. And why there? Why not the Golden Gate Bridge? Plus, he went through the railing with some force."

"He could have run toward it."

"Backward?" she asked.

After a bit of quiet while I absorbed her comments, I asked, "You think Madeline did it?"

"I don't know why she'd want to kill David. It would put everything she might be doing on her computer in danger." Hadley shook her head.

"You wanted it to be her, didn't you?" I said.

"I don't think she believes the laws that apply to other mortals apply to her," she said.

"Or that you are smart enough to catch her if they do."

Hadley smiled.

She had a charming side, I thought. No doubt Madeline had one as well, or she couldn't have gotten as far as she had. She just didn't need to use it when dealing with the unwashed masses.

In my world, logic rules. It may be boring, but it has its good points. There are limited possibilities in accounting. In the end either things add up or they don't. In murder cases, there are often unlimited possibilities. And at the moment what we had was a homicide, not an error on the ledger sheet.

Was David killed by a jealous lover? Or was it a mugging gone wild? Was it the result of a psychopath who didn't need a reason or had one we could never comprehend? A case of mistaken identity—an accident the doer didn't want to own up to? A wild animal that had disappeared in the bay?

Maybe an ingenious suicide? All were possible. And in this case, it would probably never add up—not without reasonable doubt, that is.

And unless David was messing around with the accounts, my skills were as useless as an electric blanket in hell. All this drifted through my mind as I sought sleep.

I woke up more positive and with my imagination in check. I called Mr. Lehr and attempted to withdraw. He wouldn't have it. Worse, he said he was going to call the chief of police to make sure I was part of the case. His fellow board members wanted this wrapped up quickly and completely. Even if I couldn't really help the police, I could keep him, and those with whom he chose to confide, informed.

EIGHT

Madeline's office door was closed. I found my way to Emelio's office. He was polite, but not happy to see me.

"As you might imagine, we're in a bit of turmoil here. Madeline's gone missing for the moment, thank God, but I'm having to deal with all the calls. There's insurance. The police. And while it might seem cold, I have to find a replacement for David. I posted his job on the internet this morning when I got in. I already have hundreds of résumés."

"I'll leave you alone," I said, backing out of his office. I stopped. "Why didn't you tell me you were in this country illegally?"

He reacted as if I had slapped him. He stood, went behind me, shut the door. His face was ashen.

"I've told no one," I said.

"But?" he said.

"But you are providing me with sketchy background. You said you were a qualified accountant. Not quite true. You said you had a green card. You also implied that Patrick helped on the mortgage of your new home, yet the title is in your name only."

"At his request. What's so difficult about that?"

"Very trusting on his part."

"We do trust each other. He is high up in the Roman Catholic Church. We are being cautious. At some point, when the church comes to its senses about same-sex marriage, we plan to marry, and it won't matter whose name is on the title."

"What if you have a disagreement?" I asked, wondering if there was something more that might spill out given his emotional state.

"Why, I'll just kill him, won't I? That's where this is going, isn't it?"

Marge was in the large conference room with a bunch of people in suits, rolling out blueprints. Vanessa was leading a small group through the empty venue space. Craig was with them.

I followed them at a discreet distance. These were potential customers, yet she, not Craig, seemed to be the one selling them, trying not to lose the deal. Certainly she was the one answering their questions.

I had no idea how long they'd be. I decided to leave and find a place for coffee.

I ran into Hadley at the door. She wore her gray suit and white shirt under a black trench coat. So much for not being a uniformed officer.

She was angry. She pulled me outside. We stood at the edge of the pier, not far from where the body had floated. Salty, wet air blew in our faces.

"I'm told I have to put up with you," she said.

"There are worse things," I said.

"I see we are not going to agree on a whole lot." She gave me that practiced cop look. It was supposed to intimidate me. It did. A little.

"I'm just doing what I'm told, same as you," I said.

We stood face to face. Water lapped against the pilings. A ship's horn sounded in the distance. Seagulls screeched. The morning fog was beginning to lift. A ferry crossed just beneath it.

"He was held under or possibly pulled under," she said.

I must have looked confused.

"David," she said. "No blunt force. Only bay water in his lungs."

She looked at me. My turn. I still didn't want to rat Emelio out on his immigration status. It wasn't all sympathy for Emelio. I just didn't want to see him deported before this mess could be sorted out. I told her about Emelio's nice house instead, and that it was pretty nice given his pay grade. And about Patrick.

She gave me a puzzled look.

"All the accounting is computerized. Emelio had access to the system," I said.

"Your heart isn't in this," she said.

"The foundation runs standard, proven, accepted accounting programs. Once a year a team of highly professional accountants audits the books. They know the programs. They know the scams."

"David worked for Emelio," she said.

"Yes. But as the IT guy, David worked with everyone. He was specially selected as an aid to the lovely Madeline and her two laptops. Though, like most of us, she has only one lap."

Hadley appeared to be doing some active thinking. I continued.

"Marge does the triathlon every year. In addition to running and bicycling untold miles, she swims to San Francisco from Alcatraz."

Hadley's eyebrows rose involuntarily.

"I can be valuable," I said.

"Anything else?"

"I'm checking the bank balances of the prime suspects."

"How do you know where they bank?"

"Paychecks are automatically deposited. I just follow the routing numbers. Of course, it won't show other accounts at other banks. But eventually money from various sources would be funneled into the account used to pay bills and debt. We find that first bank, we can find the others."

Two things occurred to me at that moment. The first was that any unauthorized transactions were probably transferred directly to an account without a check being requested or written. However, even electronic transfers to someone other than a legitimate business would have shown up in the audits. I had found no evidence of that.

The second thought wasn't fully developed, but if there were some funny financial goings-on, the process had to be more sophisticated. It had to be set up to bypass any recording of the transaction. Invisible. If that was the case, then surely David's involvement would be necessary. It was unlikely that any of my suspects could have done it alone. Killing, yes. Embezzling, no.

Maybe I was getting somewhere. I had to get Madeline's computers, both of them.

I had to find out more about David. His bank account showed he was struggling a little. It began when his roommate moved out. There was no sign of unexpected deposits. He had automatic bill payments set up for gas, electric and the Internet. In short, David was a dull boy. Nothing out of the ordinary. There were phone calls to and from Baltimore—his former roommate or family, I assumed. I planned to check it out. Maybe he had told someone something.

The following morning I was in Madeline's office shortly before Inspector Hadley arrived. Madeline denied running her consulting business from the foundation office. She insisted that her husband was running it without her. She was insulted that I asked.

When I asked her about the special and expensive soundproofing, she had an explanation.

"I was hired to do a full makeover of this place. No doubt heads were going to roll. A lot of people would be hurt. Things can get emotional in those circumstances, and strategies might have to be discussed in secret."

"Whose heads were on the chopping block?" I asked.

"That's none of your business."

"Okay," I said, "but you realize it might be of interest to homicide?"

She shrugged. Fiddled with her bracelets. Her apparent boredom was theatrical.

"Emelio told me none of this," I said. "He was both the finance director and in charge of human resources as well."

"So?" She had a way of making one feel like an idiot for even asking a question.

"So wouldn't he have to be involved if you were making big changes?"

She smiled. "I told him nothing. If I told Emelio anything, it would be tweeted to the world within seconds."

"Is the board aware of your grand plan?" I asked.

"The board will not be a problem."

"You're good at keeping secrets?"

That's when Hadley knocked. She didn't wait for permission to enter.

"To what do I owe this intrusion?" Madeline asked.

"I've come to pick up your laptops," Hadley said.

Madeline looked at me as if this was my doing. It was.

"You have wasted the taxpayers' money. You can't have them."

"These pieces of paper say that I can," Hadley said.

Madeline reached for her phone. "We'll see what my lawyer has to say about it."

Hadley plucked the phone from Madeline's hand. "That too."

"This is outrageous." Madeline stood. "The law doesn't permit this. I won't allow it."

"Apparently, you are a very special lady," Hadley said. "Are there any laws that *do* apply to you?"

"Gravity," Madeline said.

"Good to know," Hadley said, handing me the phone and gathering up the two laptops.

I left, following Hadley, feeling secure in the knowledge that the inspector was armed. I could feel daggers from Madeline's cold, steely eyes between my shoulder blades.

NINE

I spent the afternoon and evening going over everything. Hadley had shared what the police found on David's computers. There was no money trail leading to David, although he could have been paid in cash and buried it in a can somewhere. There was no evidence that he had bought things he couldn't afford. No curious communications on his computer or cell.

There was no evidence that anyone was involved in his death. No marks on the body to suggest David had been knocked out or subdued. Nothing under his fingernails to suggest he'd resisted.

Like me, poor David had led a pretty boring life. Unlike me, he didn't seem to have had any bad habits. He had some video games. He'd googled pizza places and brew pubs. He read sci-fi and was a fan of various superheroes and movies featuring them. He didn't seem to have had a personal life. No relationships. He was a nerd. It didn't fit for him to be into anything illegal—certainly not seriously illegal. From what I had learned from others in the office, he wasn't high on ambition nor did he have the American instinct for greed. The only thing that popped out was that he seemed to get excited by a challenge. The tougher the problem, the more excited he became. He'd spend hours—off the clock, if necessary—to solve computer problems for staff, whether they were work related or personal.

Madeline's problems were that she was keeping her personal business alive while sleepwalking through her job as executive director. She might be immoral, but she kept everything just inside the terms of the contract. The idea of murder probably wouldn't bother her, but it would be outside her comfort zone. She also used David for her personal business. One might say she misused funds or engaged in minor fraud perhaps. But again, this was a firing offense, not a criminal one. Getting fired was part of her plan anyway. Surely she wouldn't kill David over some low-level crime, even if she were morally and physically capable. What was she really hiding?

TEN

Emelio stood in the doorway, my doorway, the one to my home. The darkness was behind him. My porch light lit Emelio's forlorn face. His neck was wrapped in an oversized scarf. His eyes were sad, downcast. If it weren't for the five-o'clock shadow he would have looked like a street orphan from a Dickens novel.

"May I come in?"

I stepped aside.

My stepparents would never have forgiven me if I had sent him away, which was what first came to mind.

"Please," I said. I'm pretty sure coldness remained in my voice.

"I'm sorry," he said, unwrapping himself. "I had to talk to you."

"All right."

"Are you in the middle of something?"

"Just a glass of Cabernet. Would you like one?"

"That would be fabulous," he said with no fabulousness in his voice.

"I'm out on the deck. No wind on that side of the house. Should be warm enough. Go on out, and I'll join you."

"You have a better view than I do," he said, accepting the glass I brought him and staring out at the city skyline.

"No fog," I said. "All is pretty clear tonight."

"Yes," he said quietly. He had something on his mind, and I was glad we were going to get to it quickly. He leaned against the rail. The pockets on his Navy pea coat bulged. I hoped he wasn't carrying a gun.

"I'm frightened, Peter." He spoke as if we'd been close friends for years. I waited for him to continue. "I couldn't make it if I had to go back."

"It's not my job to round up undocumented immigrants. I have no legal or moral cause to do so. Stop worrying."

"They would kill me."

"Who's *they*?"

"I can't tell you."

"That's fine. I wouldn't believe you anyway."

He turned completely to face me. The light caught his face. So hurt. So sad.

"You said you received your accounting credentials in the UK. You did not."

"We've been over that. I know what I'm doing," he said.

"I don't doubt that. Perhaps more than most certified public accountants. But you lied. About that, about the green card and about Patrick helping you with your mortgage."

"I never said his name was on it."

"Or on the other multimillion-dollar homes you own in the city."

"It's cold out here," he said, walking inside. He took a sip of his wine and appeared to be weighing some heavy thoughts.

Perhaps he wanted to shoot me without the neighbors witnessing the act. Maybe he didn't have a gun but wanted to get closer to the kitchen and a meat cleaver.

"It's not what you think," he said. "I haven't been embezzling from the Black Tortoise Foundation."

"I'm sure that's true. No matter how talented you are, there's no way to get that kind of money from the foundation without it showing. But you've lied about so much."

"That's why I came here tonight. I wanted to get it all out. With David's death and the investigation, other things, embarrassing things, might surface." He gave that vulnerable little-orphan look. "I have no one but you—"

"And Patrick."

"—and Patrick to turn to, and I'm not sure he would understand. You can see I'm on the verge of losing everything. And only you can help me."

"Emelio?" I waited until he was fully focused on what I had to say.

"What?" he asked.

"There is no Patrick."

I'll give Emelio credit. He knew just how far to take it. And he knew when it was over. It became clear to me that Emelio was afraid his whole world would collapse. That in a homicide investigation, the police would dig into everything. My question continued to be, had David known too much? And, in connection with Emelio's hidden wealth, did I?

Yet I am a curious fellow. And I still didn't know enough to satisfy my curiosity. How could someone like Emelio have title to more than several million dollars' worth of real estate?

"My family," he said, "is part of a drug cartel. I'm helping them launder money through the buying and selling of real estate. I don't own those houses. The cartel does. My house is my take." He sighed. "There it is."

"Did they kill David because he found out?"

"No. Not that they wouldn't kill him, or me, or"—he glanced at me—"anyone who threatened their freedom or livelihood."

Emelio shook his head. "He knew nothing. And there was no way for him to find out. This wasn't connected to the foundation in any way."

"He knew a lot about computers. Suppose…"

"David knew about computer hardware. He knew how to set up the physical systems, networks, equipment, hard drives and cables. He knew very little of programs."

"Madeline seemed to think he did."

Emelio laughed. "She didn't know what an average three-year-old knows. She once kept going in circles in a parking lot because the voice on her car's GPS system kept telling her to turn left at the next opportunity. He helped her download apps, set up bookmarks and remember passwords."

"Anything else?"

"What do you mean?"

"Undo any more lies before I find them myself."

"The way I grew up…I was never bullied. I might have been small and effeminate, but I could be nasty. I had a reputation. Nobody crossed me more than once." He smiled. His eyes grew cold. "Family trait."

He downed the last of the wine in his glass and headed toward the door. "Peter?"

"Yes?"

"I didn't murder David. I'm not stealing money. Keep my secrets." He went to the door, exited with a bit of a flourish, but stopped just before disappearing. "Don't forget to lock up." He pulled his hands out of his coat pockets. Gloves, not guns. Even so, *lock up* wasn't friendly advice.

I don't think he understood the mistake he'd made with the threat. I wasn't going to take any action on his citizenship. And I was thinking about just staying out of this possible money-laundering situation if it had nothing to do with the foundation. Given that everything he'd ever told me was a lie, I could easily make a fool of myself. I feared I could do that without taking further risks. All I could really do was what I was hired to do. That is to deal with foundation issues, not with any unrelated actions of its staff, no matter how dicey. His lies and threats, however, freed me from any sympathy or loyalty I might otherwise have felt. I have no need to protect Emelio or his identity, whatever it was.

The morning brought Hadley as well as the fog. The fog would go away. Hadley probably wouldn't. We stood by her unmarked but hardly anonymous police car.

"Nice house," she said, making it sound like an accusation. She sipped coffee from a paper cup.

"I used to think of it as my hideaway. Have you been on the stakeout long?"

"Where are you headed?" she asked.

"I never got to complete my talk with Mad Madeline. After that, as far as I'm concerned, I'll write a report for my client and move on."

"Conclusions?"

"Unless Madeline's answers change how I am thinking, it's over for me. If I can't find any evidence of accounting crimes. I've done what I was hired to do."

"And the murder?" she asked, smiling.

"Murder isn't my business."

"No severe marks on his body," Hadley continued, despite my attempts to express disinterest, "except for the marks indicating he went backward through the railing. And the bruises on the shoulder, suggesting he was forcibly held underwater by someone stronger than he was."

"Two of them then?" I suggested.

"Could be one. Someone pushes him in and jumps in after. We spent more time on his laptop. In addition to the video games, he did visit some porn sites. Mild. Conventional man-woman stuff made by professionals. Emails to friends back home. Almost too ordinary."

"Too ordinary?" I asked.

"Most people have some kind of obsession, some intense interest. David led one of the most vanilla lives I've ever investigated. Okay, I've spilled my guts. Your turn," Hadley said.

I shrugged.

"You had a visitor last night," she said.

"You do have me staked out."

She smiled.

I told her everything. Had Emelio not threatened me, I might have kept some things to myself. But if I died, I thought, I wanted the facts out there. I'm not naturally vindictive, but threats of death bring out the worst in me.

When I was done with the story of Emelio's visit, she again asked me where I was going.

"I never did get that interview with Madeline."

It was not a good morning. The sky was dark, clouds swollen with rain. The morning was still steely gray when I arrived at the Fog City Arts Center and the foundation offices. A light rain fell. On the street I ran into Vanessa. She got out of a black BMW, opening a big pastel-colored, polka-dot umbrella more suited to LA than San Francisco.

I was pretty sure it was Jorge Medina, Emelio's dream guy, behind the wheel. He was wearing a slick, dark rain poncho, and the hood was pulled up over his face. He either didn't see me or didn't recognize me from Emelio's party. Or maybe he was in no mood to be civil. All three were plausible. Vanessa gave me a glance without a show of recognition, let alone a greeting.

The outer office was cold and damp. Marguerite was not happy to see me either. I watched her disappear into her office. Craig was setting out a box of beignets. He announced he'd picked them up at Brenda's, a Louisiana-oriented restaurant, on his way to work. I leaned into Emelio's office. He refused to look at me.

"I'm looking for Madeline," I said anyway.

"She's onstage."

"Onstage?" I asked, not quite grasping he meant exactly what he said.

"She's suffering in the theater."

By the time I got to Madeline, I was in no mood to dance around people's moods.

The theater was dark. The stage was lit by a shadeless floor lamp, the traditional way to keep people from falling off the edge of the stage. There were two upholstered armchairs facing each other near the lamp. In one of them sat Madeline, puffing away on a cigarette. The other chair was empty.

"Isn't smoking illegal in here?" I asked, climbing the stairs to the stage.

"There is a waiver for theatrical productions." She didn't look at me either. I could develop a complex.

"Probably just during performances."

"Your point being?"

"May I?" I asked as I moved toward the other chair. I sat. I could see her clearly, as I could the first few rows of empty seats.

The small circle of light created an intimate line of vision with nothing to distract us from each other.

"We have an author interview here tonight," she explained. "You are sitting in her chair. "If only you were that interesting."

"Just a few questions. You are the interesting one at the moment."

"Am I subject to torture for the rest of my life?" she asked, her face looking like she had just bitten into a dill pickle.

"I'm not that bad, am I?"

"I've had worse curses. You're more of a gnat than a bumblebee. What do you want?"

"To finally finish our talk."

"I would think a murder would trump any ill-founded suspicion of embezzlement," she said.

"It works the other way, Madeline. I had wrapped it up until David was found floating in the bay."

"Nothing breaks my way, it seems."

"You don't seem to be too concerned about David."

"It's a tough life," she said. "People come, people go. Some stay too long." She gave me half a smile and took a drag from her cigarette.

"You two were close. He helped you with your digital inadequacies."

"He was paid well to do so."

"To help you with your personal business? You were handling a lot of personal business on foundation time, weren't you?" I asked, filling in the hostile silence.

"I'm afraid you have me confused with an hourly worker, Mr. Strand."

"Oh no, you are a visionary who presides over an operation where expenses increase and revenue goes down. A decent business course might advise you to do that the other way around."

"Why don't you go back to your petty little bean-counting world and let the adults do the serious work?"

"As you did with that grand old theater you ran back east?"

"We were well respected nationally. Every major star came through there," she said.

"Until it was closed down for funny finances."

"None of that had anything to do with me. Like most arts organizations, we needed some funding. We were absolutely vital to that little town, the only thing that put it on the map. The mayor, who was desperate to keep us there, helped with a grant that turned out to be part of a questionable deal. I had nothing to do with it."

"A chunk of that grant was to provide you with a big bonus."

"It was investigated. The mayor went to jail. I was not charged. I wouldn't do anything illegal. Ever. Not because I am a good or moral person, but because I could not stand a moment in prison. I could not survive in there with my skills." She laughed. "My style of intimidation wouldn't work in prison." She flicked an ash and stared out into the vast, empty space. "Are you too young to understand? Has your life been so easy? Getting through until the end means being the smartest, the toughest. Otherwise you will be left along the way, and if not devoured, then tossed aside like a broken umbrella. I have a family. I am the provider." She smiled with a manufactured haughtiness one could have seen from the back row. "I use what skills I have to hide, attack—"

"Kill," I said.

"Killing is illegal. Your time is up, Mr...."

"Strand," I said, to end her fake forgetfulness. "Be happy to go, but first a compliment. You've put the screws to the Black Tortoise Foundation in a way that would inspire scam artists everywhere. They paid for your move out here to escape your past. And when you are discovered to be incompetent—and you will be—you will leave with a fortune. Much smarter than simple theft."

"I will survive. Do what I have to do, be who I have to be. Will you?"

It was a good question. I left, headed toward the lit hallway. I looked back. She continued to sit, exhaling puffs of smoke that disappeared up into the darkness.

The door to the box office, a small room, was open. Craig was inside, fumbling around with a laptop.

"Getting ready for tonight's show?" I asked.

"Oh!" he said, startled. "Just checking sales for tonight."

"It's all on there?"

"Yes," he said. He looked up. He was happy. "Going to be a sellout, looks like."

"That makes a difference to you?"

"We get a fee for running the box office, and a cut. The bigger the turnout, the bigger the cut."

"How is the money handled?"

"It isn't. At least, not by hand. It's all electronic and automatic. The fee was paid up front with rent. Box-office receipts are transferred to our clients' bank accounts. Minus our cut, which is automatically transferred to our bank account. Prevents human error and human greed. Website operations with charge cards and electronic funds transfer."

He seemed satisfied.

"No human intervention?" I asked.

"Set up once. We just plug in the variable information with each new client, and it runs like a top. Used to be that book-keeping was the hard part. Now it's just a flick of the switch."

"Same for every client? It doesn't have to be reprogrammed?"

"No," Craig said. "Ticket prices may be changed, or the ticket prices might vary depending on day or time, but the percent-ages remain the same. Genius."

"What are you two plotting?" Vanessa asked with a grin. She squeezed into the small space, her body brushing mine slowly and a little too sensuously to be an accident.

"Mr. Strand is interested in how the box office works," Craig said.

"Peter. Call me Peter," I said.

"I certainly will," Vanessa said. "And you told him all about it, did you?" she asked Craig.

"Just what I knew," he said.

"It's magic, I understand," I said.

***

I stopped by Marguerite's office. She was having a gruff conversation with one of her maintenance workers. She dismissed him when she saw me.

I explained what I wanted. She considered it. She nodded.

I had to trust someone. And if my suspicions were right, she'd be the least likely person to be involved. Although she *was* the most qualified to deal with the cold water of the bay.

Vanessa was in Emelio's doorway as I headed out. They were having an animated conversation.

⸻

I called Hadley from the dry, warm Embarcadero Hyatt lobby. There was some sort of convention going on—a big mystery writers' convention, I found out later. Strange-looking people, these writers and their fans. Maybe they could figure this out.

"Could you make sure everyone in the foundation office knows there will be a computer expert coming tomorrow afternoon? That they will be coming to examine the servers and all activity connected to the box office and all electronic transfers of money."

"And who would that be?" Hadley asked.

"Doesn't matter. Nobody is going to show up."

"You going to let me in on this?'

"I just did. Make sure everyone gets the message as soon as possible. More tomorrow." If I told her what I knew and what I believed, she would want—demand, probably—the police to handle it. In this case, the less they knew, the less they could screw it up.

"Did I somehow forget I was working for you?" she asked.

"If this works, I can give you the killer and all the proof you need by midmorning tomorrow."

"And if you can't?"

"We won't have lost ground."

"How can I argue with that?"

"Yes. See how easy it is for us to work together?" I asked.

"This is your idea of working together?"

I didn't answer.

"Don't do anything stupid," she said and disconnected.

I had every intention of following her advice. But sometimes we don't know we are doing something stupid. If we did know, we wouldn't do it. Yet stupid stuff happens.

Morning turned into afternoon. I went to the gym. I went to Dog Eared Books on Castro. Before heading up the Saturn Steps to my home, I picked up half a roasted chicken and a bottle of pinot noir. There was no work to do on the case. I had set things in motion. I had until morning for my plan to play out. It seemed like an eternity, certainly enough time to relax.

ELEVEN

I'm not sure what woke me. It was dark. I had been in a deep sleep. Must have been the wine. I'd finished the bottle. I couldn't move my hands or feet. I was bound to my big brass bed. When I tugged at what bound me, the sound was metal on metal. Handcuffs.

"Do you always sleep in the nude?" a woman asked.

"I wasn't expecting company," I said, trying to place the voice.

"I'd probably be naked if I *were*," she said.

117

The light beside the bed went on, spilling some light into the room. The voice belonged to Vanessa. So, I assumed, did the naked body with the blond hair. I would not know if she was a bottle or a natural blond. But that seemed less a problem than the butcher knife she held in her hand.

"You have a girlfriend?" she asked.

"No."

"A boyfriend?"

"No."

"Well," she said, sitting in a chair by the door to the deck. "Tell me about yourself. Tell me about your life."

"It's not very interesting," I said.

"You haven't a clue, do you? The more you talk, the longer you live."

"I was born on a cold day in a cabin in the mountains," I told her, preparing to tell her the longest tale I could.

"In China?" she asked.

"Arizona. The snowflakes, I was told, were as big as half-dollars."

"There are mountains in Arizona?"

"I think they are still there."

"I mean, I want to know about you, what makes you tick, what you want out of life, who you are, who you really are. Down deep in your soul. This is your chance at a kind of confession where you will take your secrets with you. Who would I tell?" She seemed to take some sort of pride in her logic.

"I don't know what to say."

"Did you know you snore?"

"No, I didn't."

"You haven't been around much, have you?" she asked. "If you slept with more people, someone would have told you."

"You have some advice for me?"

"You're catching on. Okay, you're young—you should get out more.

Do things. Find out who you are and find a purpose."

"Wise advice," I said. Lying was the least of my sins.

She stood again, came toward me, perched her warm, slender body on my belly.

"You're put together pretty well," she said. A sliver of light flashed on the blade of the knife. The weapon was from my kitchen. I supposed I should be grateful it wasn't the meat cleaver.

"So are you. You are the most beautiful naked woman I've ever seen." It was true, but it also seemed like the right thing to say given the circumstances. "David probably couldn't resist you. You had him come over, maybe sit on the top rail. He made it easy for you to just push him in, and your friend Jorge was there, waiting in the water below to finish the job."

"You do have a clue," she said. "I thought you only knew about the program.

You shouldn't have been so nosy," she said, putting the tip of the knife against the tip of my nose.

"If you hadn't killed David, I'd have been long gone, and your scheme would have worked forever. The auditors didn't know there was a scheme, and I didn't either. Apparently, the only one who could have known was David."

"Even he didn't know he knew, but he knew enough to blow it. He helped Jorge even though he didn't know what Jorge was doing. Pure genius, my Jorge, and a whole lot more. Anyway, it was kind of like a perpetual money machine, Jorge said, and this was merely the prototype, the test model."

"Killing me will only bring more attention," I said.

"What?" She smiled, her left hand behind her, fondling me, while her right hand, her knife hand, ran the blade along my neck and across my throat. "A little kinky sex that got out of hand." She was drawing blood. "That's all it was. Who knows who you were screwing around with."

She scooted back, the warmth of her body doing things to me despite the rush of fear. "I take a shower here to wash off any blood splatter. So I'm clean should the investigation even come close to me. My cell phone is at my place. So is Jorge's. So they can do that tracking thing, and they'll think we were there all night. We are each other's alibi."

I needed a little more time to figure out how to get out of this mess before she killed me. A distraction. The night before, I'd thought about Emelio and Madeline, both of whom seemed most likely to be players. Emelio wanted respect. He wanted people to think he had achieved a level of success—a loving relationship, a home and a respectable job. Madeline, it seemed to me, wanted complete control of her environment, which also meant the people in it. Marguerite wanted to do good work, to believe that her life contributed something to the world. Craig just wanted to keep his head above water, to make it from day to day. What they all wanted was to survive, not only physically but psychologically They wanted to protect who they were or who they thought they were.

I did too. Only the physical had the highest priority at this moment.

"What do you want out of life?" I asked Vanessa. She remained astride me, the knife running along the contours of my body. The act was strangely sensuous.

"My, my," she said. "Are you aware you are only moments from your death? Are you sure this is what you want to talk about?" I could feel the warmth of my blood on my neck.

"You brought it up, and I can't think of a better time—for you, anyway." What I was actually thinking about was how the bed was constructed. It had been a couple of years since I'd put it together. But essentially it was made of brass tubes that slid into each other. The horizontal bars running across the top of the headboard were solid brass.

"Sure, let's talk about you. What do you want out of life?" I asked again.

"To live!" she said breathlessly. "To experience what it means to live before I shrivel up and die."

"Is this part of living?" I asked.

"Only a very few have this kind of experience," she said. "We're sharing this moment, Peter."

It struck me that all I needed to do was grab the top rail, the one my hand-cuffs were attached to. If I yanked it hard enough, I could pull it completely free.

"This is perfect," she said. "Pushing poor David into the bay wasn't all that exciting. I had no sense of participation. I could not feel his death. There was nothing real about it. This is real." She was ecstatic, almost in another world.

I understood what she said. Living had never felt more vivid to me either. Everything—breath, sweat, pain, touch— was incredibly sensuous. The blade just below my navel pressed hard. The blood was hot on my flesh.

I moved my hands to the extent that I could, so the pressure on the brass bar would have equal force on the right and left. I did so slowly and grasped the bar with both hands.

"How many people go through life without ever experiencing this?" she said.

"I'm lucky too. How many people die at the hands of a beautiful, naked woman?"

"You want to do it?" she asked.

"You?" I knew what she meant.

"Do I," she said. "And at that very moment of ecstasy, you take your last breath. It would be fantastic for both of us."

As she slid farther back and focused on advancing the cause, I jerked the bar straight up. In a continuous movement I arced it over my body, crashing it with all the force I could muster against her blond head. Her body flew back against the brass rails of the footboard. Already there was no life in her eyes. I removed the knife from her hand and slid it under the mattress.

I pushed her body to the floor and began to deconstruct the footboard so I could get out of the bed and find the phone.

***

"Thank God I got here before the photographer," Hadley said, glancing down at my naked body. I couldn't get dressed with my arms and legs still attached to parts of the bed. Vanessa had used police cuffs. Hadley unlocked them. I slipped on a robe.

"She's dead, you know," Hadley said.

"Yes, I checked. I would have called 9-1-1."

"Ever kill anybody before?" she asked. Vanessa lay crumpled on the floor by the sliding doors.

"No. It's rarely called for in my line of work."

"You okay?" she asked.

"I had to do it," I said.

"It's a human instinct to protect oneself."

"Or who we think we are," I said.

"The crime-scene people will be here soon. Tell me what happened."

"You might want to put a car out in front of the foundation offices and detain anyone leaving."

"Anyone being...?"

"His name is Jorge Medina, and he'll have some sort of microprocessor on him. Important evidence."

"That's what you were going to give me later today?" she asked, pushing a button on her phone.

"Yes, I didn't anticipate…"

"…the kinky sex?"

"Any of this. I've never killed anything," I said, not sure why I was still talking.

TWELVE

I told her everything and used the rest of the morning to write up a report for Mr. Lehr. I emailed him a copy and printed ones out for Emelio, Madeline and Hadley. I called my housekeeper and provided some instructions and packed for the weekend.

Madeline was out on the pier, smoking and talking on her phone. I set her copy on her desk on my way to Emelio's office. He was there. He didn't look at me at first, and then he couldn't take his eyes off me.

I explained how Vanessa and Jorge had used a personally designed app to interrupt the box-office process. This allowed them to siphon off revenue from ticket sales. A percentage of the money was moved from the system at the time of purchase, before it was applied to the foundation's account. And all reports with regard to the transactions were altered to back up the manipulated amount of total receipts. This applied to theater events held in the larger venues, and to the larger ticket items for special events. The siphoned money went to the criminals' accounts at separate banks. It was all automatic, and because it was programmed, it didn't need to be changed for each new client. A perpetual money machine. As far as the auditors were concerned, the correct money went to the client and to the foundation. Reports showed that to be so, as there was no record of the diverted money. No one knew it was happening. Worse, this was merely a blueprint for what they could do as they expanded operations to other venues in San Francisco and around the country.

Emelio was still staring. He stood, looking at me closely. "What happened?"

"To my neck? Cut myself shaving."

His eyes were a soft gray. "No," he said. "What happened to you?"

"It's all here in the report," I said. Of course, not everything.

"Some people are terrified of others discovering their secrets," he said. "Some are terrified of unearthing their own."

He knew I knew what he meant. He looked sad. It wasn't an act.

I looked forward to a few days in wine country, maybe a visit to the spa, guaranteed fine food and wine. Beautiful country. A place where I could forget how it felt to be truly alive, to be me.

ACKNOWLEDGMENTS

My appreciation goes as always to brothers Richard and Ryan. A special thanks to my good friend David Anderson for his support. I also want to thank Orca editor Ruth Linka for making the words right and making the whole package come together in the exciting Rapid Reads program.

RONALD TIERNEY's *The Stone Veil* introduced semi-retired, Indianapolis-based private investigator "Deets" Shanahan. The book was a finalist in the St. Martin's Press/Private Eye Writers of America's Best First Private Eye Novel competition and nominated for the Private Eye Writers of America's Shamus Award for Best First Novel. *Killing Frost* is the eleventh in the Shanahan series. Ronald was founding editor of *NUVO Newsweekly*, an Indianapolis alternative weekly, and the editor of a San Francisco monthly. Until recently he lived in San Francisco, the setting for his Paladino and Lang series. He now lives in Palm Springs, California, where he continues to write. For more information, visit www.ronaldtierney.com.